I LIKE A WHOLE ONE

I LIKE A WHOLE ONE

MARGUERITA RUDOLPH

PICTURES BY JOHN E. JOHNSON

McGRAW-HILL BOOK COMPANY

New York • Toronto • London • Sydney

OTHER FIRST STEP BOOKS

LOOK AT ME by Marguerita Rudolph
illustrated by Karla Kuskin

MOVING AWAY by Alice R. Viklund
illustrated by Reisie Lonette

Library of Congress Catalog Card Number: 68-30566

234567890 HDBP 754321069

To my grandson, Darius

Arthur was a small boy with big round eyes and a friendly smile.

Arthur liked things to do—catching a ball, climbing a ladder, running downhill.

And he liked things to eat. He especially liked fruit.

One Saturday Arthur's uncle sent the family a beautiful basket of fruit. As soon as he came in the house, Arthur saw the basket—and the big red apples.

The apples were so smooth and shiny, and they smelled so delicious that Arthur told his mother he wanted one.

"I'll cut an apple in half for you," said his mother.
"I don't want half. I like a whole one," said Arthur.
His mother cut the apple in half just the same
because she didn't think he could eat a whole one.

"I want a whole apple," said Arthur. "Please."

"I said half," his mother reminded him. "It's close to lunch."

And his mother did not give him a whole one. So Arthur took the half apple and slowly ate all of it except the seeds, which he put in a row on the table.

At lunch time, after everybody had finished their food, Arthur's mother took a banana from the fruit basket. She stripped the peel off with her fingers and cut the banana in pieces for Arthur's dessert.

"Can I have a whole banana?" he asked. "I don't like it broken."

"But I already fixed it for you," Arthur's mother explained. "Here." And she put the dish with the cut-up banana in front of him. Then she sprinkled some crumbs of brown sugar on top.

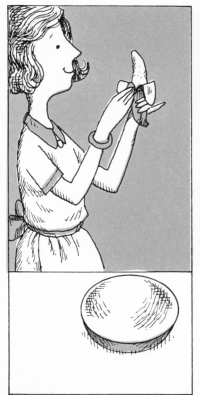

"I want a whole banana," Arthur said.

"Next time I'll remember to give you a whole banana," answered his mother. "Eat it this way now."

Arthur looked down at the circles of cut-up banana. They looked good to eat. He thought of his mother's promise to give him a whole one next time, so he changed his mind and ate his dessert. It tasted so good he licked his lips clean before wiping them with a napkin.

"I think I'll have some fruit, too," said Arthur's father, looking at the fruit basket. He picked out a speckled pear and held it up by the stem.

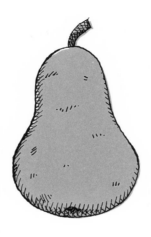

The pear was roundish, but not like an apple. It was a little long, but not like a banana. Its stem looked like a strong handle attached at the top.

"I want a pear, too," said Arthur.

"Fine," said his father, "have a piece of mine."

"I don't want a piece. I want a *whole* one!" Arthur shouted.

"I know," his father said quietly, "but you will not be able to eat a whole pear. You are too full after lunch. A small piece is enough."

"No," Arthur answered in a trembling voice. "It's not enough." Then he began to cry.

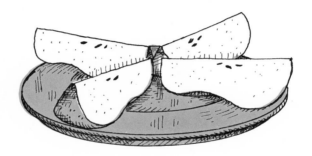

Arthur's father cut the big pear in half, then each half again in two. He put the four pieces in a circle on a plate and cheerfully passed the plate to Arthur.

Arthur wiped his tears and looked at the pieces of pear. They were white and a bit rough on the inside. The cut pear smelled sweet and spicy. Arthur would have liked to eat it, but he had already made up his mind.

"No," he said again in an angry voice. And he did not take a piece.

After lunch Arthur went to his room. He sat on the floor and played with his trucks, but he was still thinking about the fruit.

Later in the day he heard his grandmother's voice in the kitchen. Then she came and stood by the door to his room. She was a pretty lady and wore bracelets and beads and a fancy hat. She always played with Arthur when she came over, and he was glad to see her.

"What's the problem?" she asked Arthur.

Arthur did not answer.

"I hear Uncle Frank sent a basket of delicious fruit," said Grandmother, coming closer and bending down to stroke Arthur's head.

Now Arthur began to sob. He looked up at his grandmother and said, "But I want a whole one."

"A whole one?" asked Grandmother. "A whole one of what, dear?"

"Fruit," said Arthur.

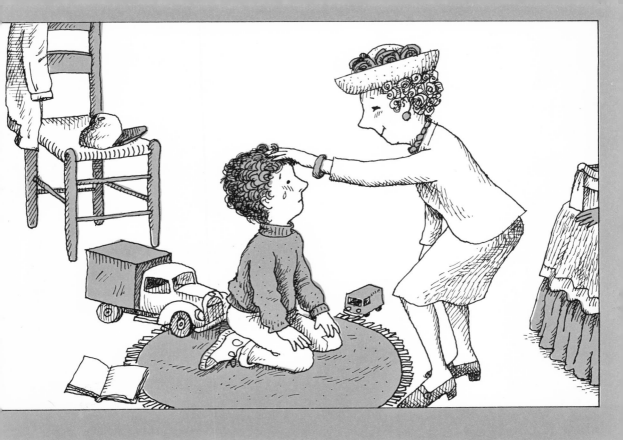

His grandmother thought a moment, then she said, "Well, you just come along with Grandma. We'll see what we can do to fix things up."

Arthur took his grandmother's hand, and they both walked into the kitchen, where Arthur's mother had just taken a cake out of the oven.

Grandmother sat down at the table and Arthur sat right next to her. In the center was the beautiful basket of fruit.

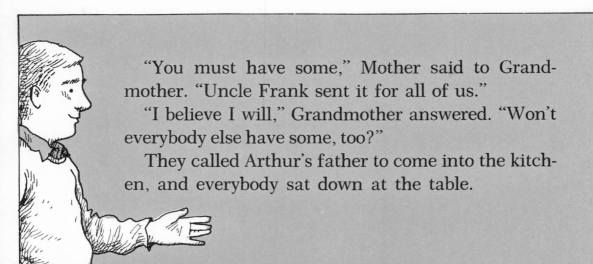

"You must have some," Mother said to Grandmother. "Uncle Frank sent it for all of us."

"I believe I will," Grandmother answered. "Won't everybody else have some, too?"

They called Arthur's father to come into the kitchen, and everybody sat down at the table.

Grandma started passing the fruit. She passed it first to Arthur—maybe because he was the smallest, or maybe because she liked him most, or maybe because he was sitting next to her.

Arthur was pleased. He looked at the basket from all sides. What will he choose? He was thinking and thinking.

His mother said: "Arthur will choose something big—like an apple."

But Arthur did not choose an apple.

His father said: "He might choose a pear—so he can have it whole."

But Arthur did not choose a pear.

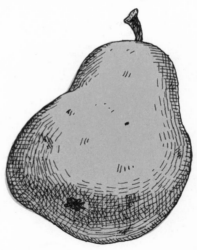

"Maybe you'd like a big banana," said Grandmother, "and you can give *me* a little piece."

Arthur looked at his grandmother and shook his head. Then he looked carefully at the basket of fruit again, and finally decided.

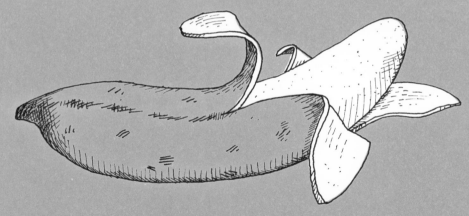

He decided to take a whole bunch of little green grapes.

"One, two, three, four . . ." he counted the grapes with his finger, turning the bunch. There were so many grapes, Arthur stopped counting!

He knew no one would cut the grapes in half, or break them in pieces. He looked happily at the whole bunch of grapes in his hands! Pop, in the mouth, and bite in. Slippery, sweet and juicy. One by one, Arthur ate them all.

"Thank you for the grapes," he said, looking at all the grown-ups with his friendly smile. His mother and father and grandmother were all very surprised. None of them had guessed what he would choose.

ABOUT THE AUTHOR

MARGUERITA RUDOLPH is director of the Great Neck Community School and has had years of experience in early childhood education. She is also the author of numerous books and articles for and about children, including *The Traveling Frog*, *How a Shirt Grew in the Field*, *The Magic Sack*, and *Look At Me*, an earlier First Step Book.

ABOUT THE ARTIST

JOHN E. JOHNSON is the illustrator of some thirty books, most of them written for children, and his art has been selected for shows by the AIGA and the Society of Illustrators.

A graduate of the Philadelphia Museum school, Mr. Johnson lives on New York's upper west side with his wife, two children, and a Bassett hound named Grover.